5-7-14

To: Ms Scholl
from Josh

# CAPTAIN AWESOME, SOCCER STAR

By STAN KIRBY

Illustrated by
GEORGE O'CONNOR

LITTLE SIMON
New York   London   Toronto   Sydney   New Delhi

 LITTLE SIMON

An imprint of Simon & Schuster Children's Publishing Division • 1230 Avenue of the Americas, New York, New York 10020 • Copyright © 2012 by Simon & Schuster, Inc. All rights reserved, including the right of reproduction in whole or in part in any form. LITTLE SIMON is a registered trademark of Simon & Schuster, Inc., and associated colophon is a trademark of Simon & Schuster, Inc. For information about special discounts for bulk purchases, please contact Simon & Schuster Special Sales at 1-866-506-1949 or business@simonandschuster.com. The Simon & Schuster Speakers Bureau can bring authors to your live event. For more information or to book an event contact the Simon & Schuster Speakers Bureau at 1-866-248-3049 or visit our website at www.simonspeakers.com. Manufactured in the United States of America 0213 MTN • 10 9 8 7 6 5 4 3
Library of Congress Cataloging-in-Publication Data
Kirby, Stan. Captain Awesome, soccer star / by Stan Kirby ; illustrated by George O'Connor. — 1st ed. p. cm. Summary: Second-grader Eugene McGillicudy finds that he can tap the power of Captain Awesome without wearing the costume, as he scores a goal for his soccer team. [etc.] [1. Superheroes—Fiction. 2. Soccer—Fiction.] I. O'Connor, George, ill. II. Title. PZ7.K633529Cak 2012 [FIC]—dc23 2011023402
ISBN 978-1-4424-4331-0 (pbk)
ISBN 978-1-4424-4332-7 (hc)
ISBN 978-1-4424-4333-4 (eBook)

# Table of Contents

CHAPTER 1

Fall Falls on
Captain Awesome

By
Eugene

# *F*ALL!

*Is there a worse name for a season than "fall"?* Eugene McGillicudy thought as he walked home from Sunnyview Elementary School where he had just escaped from second grade.

*Fall. Who names a season after an accident? Are there other seasons called "trip" or "crash" or "oops"?*

NO.

So why name it "fall"? Is it really because the leaves are turning color and falling off the trees and that snow might soon be falling from the sky?

Really? Whatever the reason, it is certainly better than "autumn."

*I'd bet no one even knows what that word means,* Eugene thought.

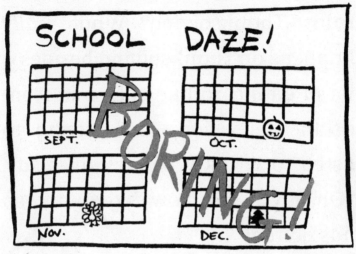

Fall was the most boring, BORING, BO-RING time of year between the start of the school year and winter break—a time when NOTHING happens.

Oh sure, you can say that

there's Halloween, but that's really only for one day and sometimes it rains. Thanksgiving? What *really* happens on Thanksgiving besides a lot of eating, falling asleep in front of the television, and having to listen to wrinkly old relatives say, "Oh, my! Look how big so-and-so has gotten!"

So yeah, there's nothing.

**KA-THUNKK!**

"OUCH!" cried Eugene, his thoughts now focused on

things hitting his
head.

*I'm under attack!*
Eugene thought and dove
for cover behind a tree.
*But who could it be?!*
**KA-THUNKK!**

"Ouch!" Something
bounced off of his
head again.

"Curse you,
Captain Ka-Thunk!
I know it's you!" Eugene
quickly poked his head out
from behind the tree and

shouted. "You'll not ka-thunk the number one fan of Super Dude without a fight!"

What's that?

You've never heard of Super Dude?

Do you live in a crater on the moon? Actually, if you've never heard of Super Dude, then you'd have to live in a crater on the *dark side* of the moon.

Super Dude is only the greatest superhero ever. He is the star of mountains and *mountains* of comic books, all of which Eugene owned.

Following Super Dude's example, Eugene created his own outfit and became . . .

## CAPTAIN AWESOME!

Along with his best friend, Charlie Thomas Jones (also known as the superhero Nacho Cheese Man), and sidekick, Turbo the Hamster, Eugene formed the Sunnyview Superhero Squad to stop evil from eviling in the town of Sunnyview. Sunnyview had a surprising amount of eviling going on.

## KA-THUNKK!

Again.

*OUCH!*

*ACORNS!*

If it wasn't Captain Ka-Thunk or his Thunkulicious Thunkers, it could only mean one thing!

High in the tree, General Squirrel Nuthatch was chittering away in his rodent language while staring angrily at Eugene. He held another Atomic Acorn in his paws.

"So, General Nuthatch, it seems you have escaped from the Nut House for evil rodents!" Eugene called up. "But it was, dare I say, *nuts* of you to return to Sunnyview to unleash your attack! You and your Atomic Acorns will be a threat to the good people of Sunnyview no longer, for you have ka-thunked the number one Squirrel Stopper in the universe!

"You've gotten a little too squirrely for your own good,

Nuthatch! There's gonna be more than leaves falling off trees this autumn!" Captain Awesome cried out in his most awesome superhero voice.

"MI-TEE!" Captain Awesome shouted as he leaped his bravest leap. . . .

CHAPTER 2

# Soccer Is the Best Season

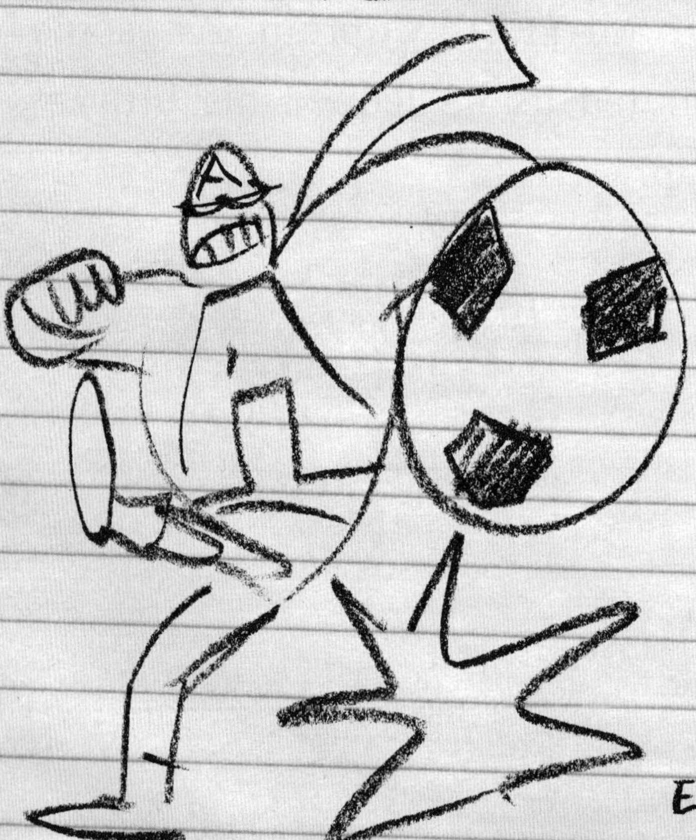

By Eugene

# KA-THUNKK!

"OUCH!" cried Eugene as something round hit him in the back of the head. Was he under attack? Again?!

Eugene looked around. What he saw was better. Much better.

It was a soccer ball, and it signaled the start of one of the classic four seasons of boyhood. Eugene knew the list by heart:

1. Christmas vacation
2. Spring break
3. Summer vacation
4. Soccer season!

"Sorry, Eugene!" It was Charlie, aka Nacho Cheese Man, the second-greatest fighter of evil in Sunnyview. "I was trying to 'bend it' like Sim Simonson, the Arctic Sharks striker, but it was more like my foot 'flopped it.'"

"Like Phillip?" asked Eugene. He pointed across the school yard where Phillip Dickenson tried to kick a soccer ball. He completely missed and flopped on to his back.

"Exactly!" Charlie said. As Phillip rolled over slowly like a roly-poly bug, Charlie pulled a flyer from his pocket. "Check *this* out."

Eugene's Awesome Vision scanned the piece of paper. It was a sign-up sheet for the Sunnyview

SUNNYVIEW
YOUTH SOCCER LEAGUE

EIGHT-YEAR-OLD DIVISION

Youth Soccer League's eight-year-old division.

"We're in!" Eugene said. "Let's sign up!"

The more Eugene thought about it, the more excited he got. By the time he got home for dinner, he was ready to pop like Colonel

Kernel, the human popcorn ball who was defeated by Super Dude in Super Dude No. 14, *Super Dude's Microwave Adventures.*

"Let this be a lesson to you, Colonel Kernel," Super Dude had said, as he tossed the puffy villain in a prison tub. "You'll never be able to defeat the rays of goodness!"

Eugene ran into the living room. "Mom! Dad! Big news! Like, it's bigger than the biggest big thing you can think of!"

Eugene closed the front door. "You're looking at the *almost*

newest member of the Sunnyview
Youth Soccer League!"

"That's a fantastic idea, son,"
Eugene's dad, Ned, said. "Will Charlie
be joining you?"

"Dad! Of course!" Eugene said.
"I'd never join a team without my
best friend."

With *two* superheroes on

Sunnyview's team, they would be unstoppable. *How long would it take to score a million goals ... every game? The soccer games would last for days! Or weeks, even!*

Eugene imagined the sounds of loud cheering.

## CHAPTER 3

# Bend It Like Awesome

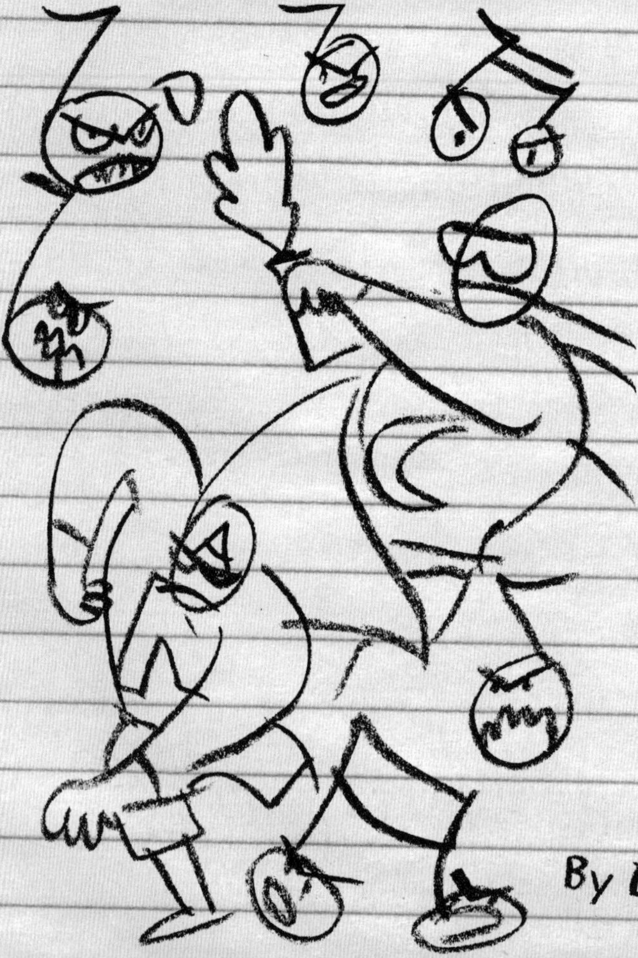

By Eugene

# Finally!

Saturday! The big, big day! The soccer team's first practice!

**_BEEP! BEEP!_**

"Dad!" Eugene gasped. "Wait!" His dad was already in the car, eager to go. "I'm coming!"

Eugene flew down the stairs, tripped over his feet, bounced off the handrail, boomed off the wall, and caught himself by jumping off

the third stair and landing on the floor below.

"MI-TEE!" Eugene yelled in his most awesome Captain Awesome voice and pointed at the stairs. "Yes! Stairs of Evil, beware! Captain Awesome shall not be tripped by you on Soccer Day!"

Once in the car, it was just a quick drive down the street to pick up Charlie, who eagerly waited on the sidewalk.

"MI-TEE!" Eugene yelled out the car window.

"Cheesy-yo!" Charlie responded, and hopped in.

"We must be on constant watch for evil," Eugene said. He scanned the passing houses as the car turned the corner. "Evil could be

lurking around any corner, behind any trash can, or inside any building or store. It could be anywhere!"

"Except for Ice Cream Coney's," Charlie reminded Eugene. "There's nothing in there but ice cream and toppings. And those are never, ever evil. Only yummy."

"Yummy," both boys said in unison.

"I know what you guys need to do!" Mr. McGillicudy blurted out.

Eugene sank a little lower in his seat, filled with the mixture of dread and embarrassment that only a parent could create. His dad was about to . . .

"Sing!" Eugene's dad continued.

"Sing a song?" Charlie asked, scrunching his nose at the thought.

"Exactly!" Ned said. "A song

will pump you guys up for your first soccer practice!"

Mr. McGillicudy turned on the car's CD player. The car filled with the hideous sounds of HORRIBLE baby music.

"I love this song!" Ned shouted and tapped his fingertips on the steering wheel.

But the stuff coming out of the car speakers was, of course, not really music, but his little sister's favorite song:

the one and only "Monday."

Eugene and Charlie were hit by every evil word.

"I like Monday, Monday, Monday.

"It's the best day, best day, best day.

"I'm so happy, happy, happy!

"It's a Monday, Monday, Monday!"

**ARGH!**

Eugene and Charlie slapped their hands over their ears!

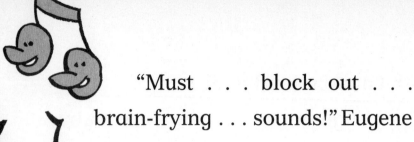

"Must . . . block out . . . brain-frying . . . sounds!" Eugene groaned.

*"Monday, Monday, Monday!"*

"Stupid . . . orange Dinosaur Delmer! Gross baby songs . . . crawling into . . . my ears . . . Head will explode like gooey . . . goo!" Charlie struggled to get the words

out before his head exploded like gooey goo.

*"I'm so happy, happy, happy!"*

"Queen Stinkypants!" Eugene gasped, referring to the secret evil identity of his baby sister, Molly. "She must've . . . planned this . . . to melt . . . our brains!"

"So we can't . . . play . . . soccer!" Charlie continued.

"Goodness and soccer shall never be . . . defeated by dino

badness and baby songs," Eugene replied. "Only one thing . . . to . . . do . . ."

"SUPER SONIC SCREAM!"

both boys shouted at the same time.

"AAAAAAAAAAAAAA
AAAAAAAAAAAAAAAA
AAAAAAAAAAAAAA
AAAAH!"

Eugene's dad turned off the CD player. "Boys! What's wrong?!" he asked urgently.

Eugene and Charlie removed their hands, relieved that the ear-melting sounds of the "Happiest Orange Dinosaur in the Happyzoic Era" had been shattered by their Super Sonic Scream.

"It's okay now, Dad." Eugene sighed. "But you have no idea how close you came to having to clean our exploded brains off the ceiling of your car."

"Exploded and *gooey* brains!" Charlie added.

Eugene's dad wasn't entirely sure what the two boys were talking about, but he had just vacuumed the car last Saturday, so he was more than happy to avoid any messes in the backseat.

Especially gooey exploded-brain messes. Mr. McGillicudy thought he would really need to scrub to get that stuff out.

# CHAPTER 4

# Soccer Practice Makes Less Than Perfect

By Eugene

"**G**o!"

Charlie and Eugene zoomed from the car the moment Eugene's dad turned off the engine at Sunnyview Park.

"Boys! Wait for—" But before Eugene's dad could finish his sentence, he was alone in the car. "—me."

"Over there!" Eugene cried, seeing some friends from Sunnyview Elementary. Evan

Mason, Mike Flinch, and Bernie Melnick were already kicking soccer balls and knee juggling.

Eugene charged to the nearest ball. With the explosive shout of "MI-TEE!" he kicked it as hard as he could. The ball zoomed over the grass and came to a stop next to the largest, pinkest blob of cotton candy Eugene had ever seen.

And then the blob moved! It kicked the ball!

*Wait a second . . .* , Eugene thought as the Annoying Little Girl Siren in his head grew louder. *That's no cotton-candy blob! Arrrgh! It's . . .*

"Well, if it isn't Stinkgene and Charleach!" Meredith Mooney yelled out. She was dressed from head-to-toe in pink, as usual, and smelled like a strawberry bathroom air freshener. "Here to impress us all with your soccer skills?"

"Shouldn't you be looking for the all-girls' cootie team, Meredith?" Eugene teased, wondering where Meredith managed to buy pink soccer shoes.

"Ha! Shows what you know, Eugerm," Meredith replied. "This is *coed* soccer. That means it's for boys *and* girls. You're on *my* team." Meredith laughed the kind of laugh that made the hair on the back of Eugene's neck stand up like the bristles of a toothbrush.

Eugene started to laugh too.

But then he realized no one else was laughing. In fact, Charlie was biting his lower lip and had a look on his face that made Eugene think he had to go to the bathroom, bad. Like really, *really* bad.

But Charlie didn't need a bathroom break. He needed a Meredith break.

"Girls?!" Charlie gasped when Marlo Craven and Sally Williams joined Meredith. "No one said there'd be girls on the team!"

"This is just a cootie festival disguised as a soccer practice," Eugene said, equally stunned. There was one person who could clear this up right away. "Where's our coach? Does he know there are girls on our team?"

**BREET-TWEET-TWEET!**

"Surprise!" said Eugene's dad. He ran onto the soccer field wearing a whistle and carrying a big net full of soccer balls.

## SHOCK AND HORROR!

"DAD?! *You're* the coach?! Wait. Did you know there were girls on the team?!" Eugene asked.

"Yeah! A coed team! Isn't it great?" Coach McGillicudy replied and dropped the soccer balls on the grass.

But this was not the worst thing that could happen. That would be a rocket ship from Dinosaurus X9 that brought the evil Super Pteranodonald to crush cars and eat Sunnyview.

Although, compared to the thought of playing soccer with Meredith, the pink cotton-candy blob, a superalien dinosaur attack didn't seem like such a bad thing after all.

"We have a lot of practicing to do," Coach McGillicudy said. "Our first big game is next week against the Westville Kickers."

"They're the best team in the league!" Mike Flinch whispered to the others.

"Yeah! I hear they've never been beaten. By anyone. EVER," Sally added.

"Now, before we get started," Coach McGillicudy started. "I've got a little surprise that I think will get everyone pumped up."

*PUMPED UP?*

Dread and embarrassment Part Two!

*Not another orange dinosaur song!* Eugene dove on the bag of soccer balls, looking for his dad's MP3 player, so he could rip out the battery pack and hide it forever.

Coach McGillicudy continued as if Eugene's behavior was the most normal thing in the world. And for Eugene, it was.

"I've got uniforms!" Coach McGillicudy proudly announced.

SUNNYVIEW
MEGABYTES

Coach McGillicudy opened a big box and pulled out a stack of bright red shirts. Team jerseys! Names and numbers were on the back. On the front was the team's name: Sunnyview Megabytes.

"Nice, huh?"Coach McGillicudy said. "The Sunnyview Megabytes! I thought of it myself!"

"What's a megabyte?" Charlie asked Eugene. "Is it evil? I can't play on an evil soccer team."

"Don't worry," Eugene replied. "It's some computer word my dad likes to say. A lot."

After they put on their new shirts, Coach McGillicudy ran the team through some soccer drills.

First was dribbling the ball. Eugene tripped over his ball and fell to the ground.

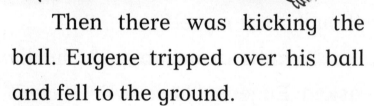

Then there was kicking the ball. Eugene tripped over his ball and fell to the ground.

And finally there was blocking the ball. The ball smacked Eugene in the chest.

And then Eugene tripped over the ball and fell to the ground.

"Okay! Let's start with some passing exercises!" Coach McGillicudy announced. "Everyone split into groups of two!"

Meredith's hand shot up quickly. "I'll pass with Charlie," she declared.

Charlie stiffened and his face scrunched up like he had to go to the bathroom again. He followed Meredith away from the group and looked back briefly to mouth the words *HELP ME!* to Eugene.

Meredith—who was secretly Captain Awesome and Nacho Cheese Man's archrival, Little Miss Stinky Pinky—was obviously up to no good. She was trying to keep the Sunnyview Superhero Squad separated so they wouldn't score their million goals!

*Typical villain,* thought Eugene. But enough is enough! Little Miss Stinky Pinky did not reckon with the soccer-powered goodness of Captain Awesome. He would never let Nacho Cheese Man be led to his

soccer-kicking defeat.

"Game on!" Captain Awesome shouted as he set to work to save Nacho Cheese Man! "Neither Stinky Pinky, nor cotton-candy blobs, nor the threat of grass stains shall stop me from scoring this gooooooaaaal for goodness!"

# CHAPTER 5

# When Blows the Whistle of Evil

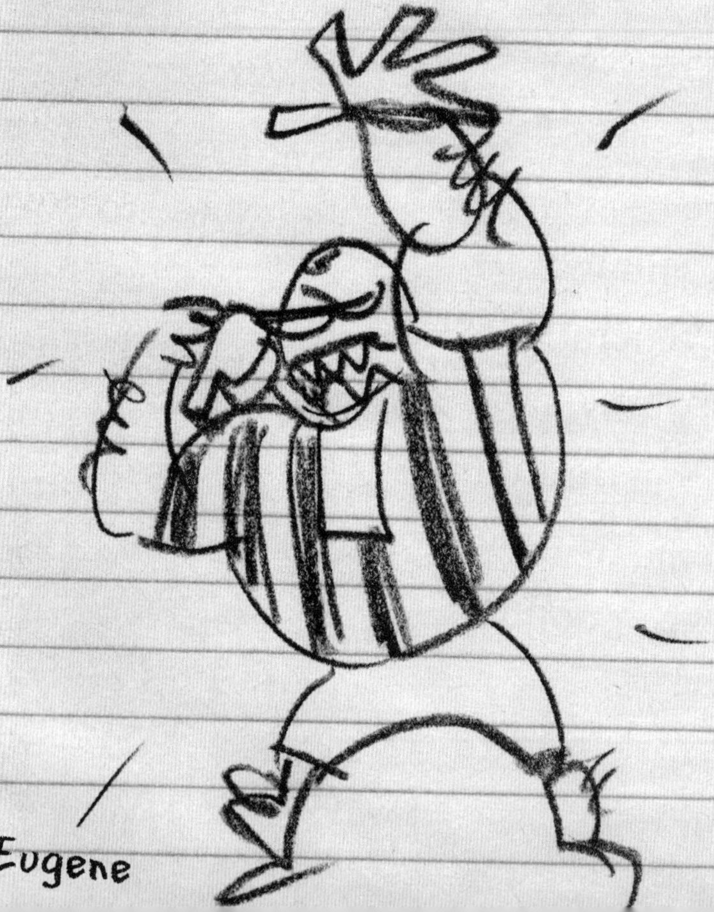

By Eugene

# Sigh.

The ride home seemed much longer than the ride to the park. Like a billion, jillion years longer. Eugene's excitement was gone, replaced by a dull disappointment in his big soccer debut. How could he score his million goals if the ball kept sneaking under his feet and tripping him?

"If only I was wearing my cape." Eugene sighed

to himself. He always thought better thoughts in a cape.

*The CAPE!*

That's when it hit him.

The idea.

*THE BIGGEST, MOST BIGGER IDEA.*

*THE AWESOMEST, MOST AWESOME IDEA, EVER!*

Yes, Eugene would absolutely

wear his Captain Awesome outfit for the first big Megabytes game next Saturday! There would be no stopping him if he played as Captain Awesome. He'd kick supergoals with his left foot and then superer goals with his right foot and then supererest goals with his left and right foot at the same time!

VICTORY!

The rest of the week was a blur of school, lunch, homework, and looking for evil. It seemed like forever for those seven days to pass, but by the next Saturday, Eugene was ready and, more importantly, so was his Captain Awesome outfit.

Eugene secretly packed it into his backpack and grabbed the Turbomobile, the clear plastic ball Captain Awesome's hamster sidekick, Turbo, used to patrol for evil.

Warm-up drills got off to a great start! Eugene only tripped over the ball twice. The ball only hit him in the head once. And that was a stray ball from the other team.

Eugene kicked it back to the Kickers and took a short break with Charlie to check them out.

"They've got matching pants," Charlie said.

"Just like the Doom Legion of

Smartypants in Super Dude No. 64," Eugene said. "We can beat these guys."

"Okay, team! Gather round!" Coach McGillicudy called out. "We've got five minutes before the game against the Kickers starts, so listen up!"

Charlie and the other members of the Sunnyview Megabytes jogged over to their coach. Everyone except for Eugene, that is.

In a flash Eugene snuck from the group, raced behind the snack shed, and unzipped his backpack! Inside lay his only hope, folded rather nicely and smelling of springtime fabric softener: his Captain Awesome outfit!

**BREET-TWEET-TWEET!**

The referee's whistle! The game was starting!

Captain Awesome zoomed from behind the snack shed and ran onto the soccer field with the most heroic run in the history of heroic running.

"Never fear, Megabytes!" Captain Awesome said. "Captain Awesome is here to lead our team to victory and score a million goals! **MI-TEE!**"

But instead of being greeted with the adoring cheers of the crowd, Captain Awesome only heard the shrill sound of **BREET-TWEET-TWEET!**

The referee held up a yellow card. "Yellow card!" he cried out,

calling the
penalty  against
Eugene. "Entering the field of play
without permission. Also wearing a
cape. No capes allowed."

Coach McGillicudy had to pull
Eugene from the field.

"But . . . but . . . I *need* my
cape!" a stunned Captain Awesome

explained. "I'm Captain Awesome!"

"I don't care if you're Santa Claus," the referee replied. "It's the rules."

Eugene looked at his dad, his friends, and finally back to the referee. And then it dawned on him. This was no ordinary soccer official. The striped shirt, the loud whistle, and the cards of yellow and red should have been clues.

*If only I hadn't been so concerned about*

scoring a million goals, I would've noticed sooner! Captain Awesome thought. Mental note: Next time only worry about scoring a half-million goals, so I can focus more on the very evil standing right in front of my face!

This "referee" was really the evil **Whistleblower**, the superannoying supervillain with his Noisy Whistle of Annoyance and Ouch-That-Hurts-My-Ears-Ness.

"Blow all you want with your mighty evil lungs, Whistleblower!"

Captain Awesome said to the villain. "Nothing shall stop Captain Awesome from scoring the winning goal for all that's good and true!"

# CHAPTER 6

## Game On!

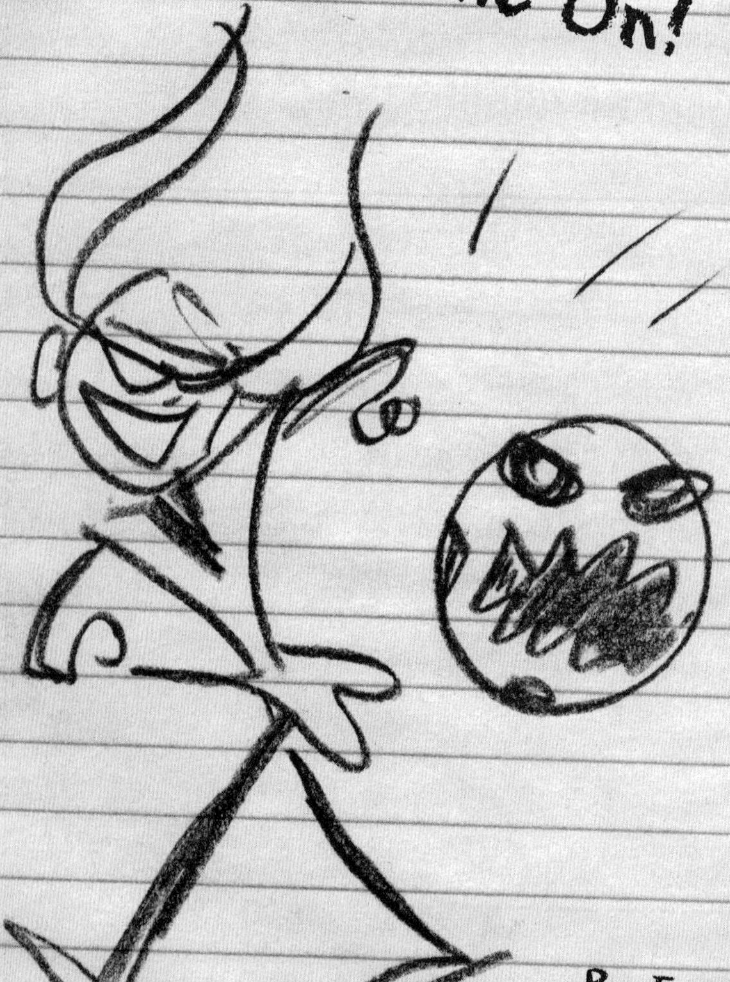

By Eugene

There's really no reason to ask who the best player was on the Sunnyview Megabytes.

"ME!" Meredith would shout before you even finished the question. And the sad thing? She was right.

Not only was Meredith the best player on the team, she was also the pinkest girl in all of Sunnyview, certainly the world, and maybe even the whole universe, including the craters of the moon.

Eugene returned after removing his Captain Awesome outfit. Wearing his regular team jersey, he joined the two teams on the field, and the Westfield Kickers captain kicked off. Meredith controlled the ball and worked it downfield, dashing and darting between the Westfield Kickers players.

"I'm open! Pass the ball!" Eugene called out.

Meredith passed the ball to

Charlie, who sent it to Marlo. She boinged it off her forehead, sending it back to Charlie who passed it to Meredith.

"Over here! Over here!" Eugene called out.

Meredith did a give-and-go with Sally, who passed the ball back, kicking it right past Eugene.

*Why won't they kick the ball to me?! What's with them?!* Eugene was frustrated. *Wait! Did I accidentally become invisible?!*

Eugene ran down the field, after the two girls, calling out, "I'm right here! I'm right here! I'm just invisible!" But then the stinky stink of something that stunk worse than not being passed the soccer ball filled Eugene's nose.

**PEE-YEW!**

"Gaaah daaah baaaah waaah!"

The evil sound of nonsense filled Eugene's ears.

*There's only one person that can sound that gobbledygooky,* Eugene realized.

There! On the sidelines! Queen Stinkypants was at it again! Her stinky diaper of evil was firing across the soccer field and caught Eugene in its awful odor! Not even the soccer fields of Earth were safe from her stink clouds and baby gibberish.

Eugene stopped. It was impossible to run with his lungs filled with Queen Stinkypants Diaper Air. He pinched his nose, squinted his eyes and . . .

**BAM!**

The next thing Eugene knew he was on the ground, flat on his back, holding his stomach.

OOF!

He'd been hit by the soccer ball. Hard. In the glare of the sun he saw the outline of two faces staring down at him. Two *very* similar faces.

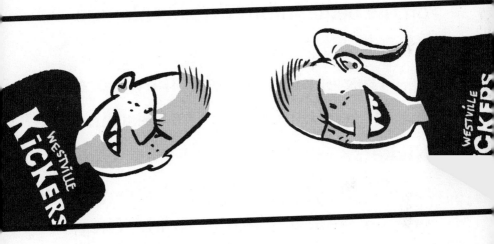

If "mean" could put on a blue jersey and play soccer for ninety minutes on Saturday afternoons, you'd have George and Lulu Morris.

Matching brown hair with pale skin and freckles, they were more like two twin bulldogs chasing an old, slobber-drenched tennis ball on the beach than two kids playing soccer.

This explained why they were the all-star players for the Westville Kickers.

"If you want to nap, I can get you a pillow!" Lulu said. They laughed and ran upfield, dribbling the ball and passing it between them.

Coach McGillicudy called a time-out and ran over to Eugene. "You want to take a break for a little bit, son?" he asked.

Eugene looked up and saw his dad's face. The sun outlined his head like a halo.

"Yeah," Eugene mumbled.

Eugene plopped on the bench next to Bernie Melnick, who had earned a reputation as one of the second grade's greatest benchwarmers.

"It's nice here on the bench, isn't it, Eugene?" Bernie asked. "This is a much nicer bench than the one for basketball, and lots more comfortable than the benches on the baseball field. Yep, for bench-sitting, the soccer field can't be beat!"

Bernie continued, completely unaware that the last thing Eugene wanted to do was to talk.

"You did pretty well against the ready-steady-kick," Bernie said.

"What do you mean?"

"The ready-steady-kick," Bernie replied. "It's the play the Morris twins are famous for. I heard from a friend of a friend of my cousin that the Morris twins once used their ready-steady-kick to knock a guy so far back in time that he became a pirate on a Spanish ship, true story!"

But Eugene didn't have time to think about the impossibility of going back through time from a soccer kick. Eugene was too busy sitting in stunned silence.

Somehow Turbo, the hamster, had rolled his Turbomobile out of Eugene's backpack and was headed into the middle of the soccer action! Turbo rolled under George's feet as he tried to pass the ball to his sister. George tripped over the Turbomobile

and crashed flat on his face.
**PLOP!**

"Ow! Muh hace! Muh hace!"
George's cries were muffled by the
grass in his mouth.

George jumped to his feet
and spit out a mouthful of turf,
totally unaware that Meredith had
sped past him. Meredith dribbled

downfield dodging the remaining Kickers. Charlie was open, and in a flash she passed the ball across the field.

"Go, Charlie, go!" she yelled. "Take it in!"

Eugene stood on the bench to  get a better view. His heart pounded in his chest! This was even better than the time Super Dude scored a touchdown as time ran out to beat the

Halftime Show-Offs in the Super Dude Bowl.

Charlie dribbled toward the goal!

"GO! GO! GO!" Eugene screamed from the bench!

Charlie faked a pass to Marlo, freezing the defender in his tracks, then unleashed a massive kick!

## *WHAM!*

The soccer ball sailed toward the net! The goalie dove! The ball skipped once on the grass and bounced off the fingers of the goalie's outstretched hands!

"GOOOOOOOOOOAL!" Eugene shouted and fell off the bench. He jumped to his feet in time to see Turbo scampering for the sidelines.

*Way to go, Turbo! Way to go, Nacho Cheese Man!* Eugene thought.

The score may have read Westville: 1, Sunnyview: 1, but in Eugene's mind it was Sunnyview Superhero Squad: 1, and Baron and Baroness Von Booger: a huge, big, fat 0.

## ZEE-RO!

And the Von Boogers weren't happy about it. The Baron glared at the Turbomobile with laserlike eyes. It was up to Eugene to rescue

his sidekick from the twin terror soccer-ball-kicking feet of the Von Boogers. He leaped from the bench and ran toward his little buddy.

"Get your laser eyes away from my hamster!" Eugene yelled.

# CHAPTER 7

# Tiebreakers of Doom

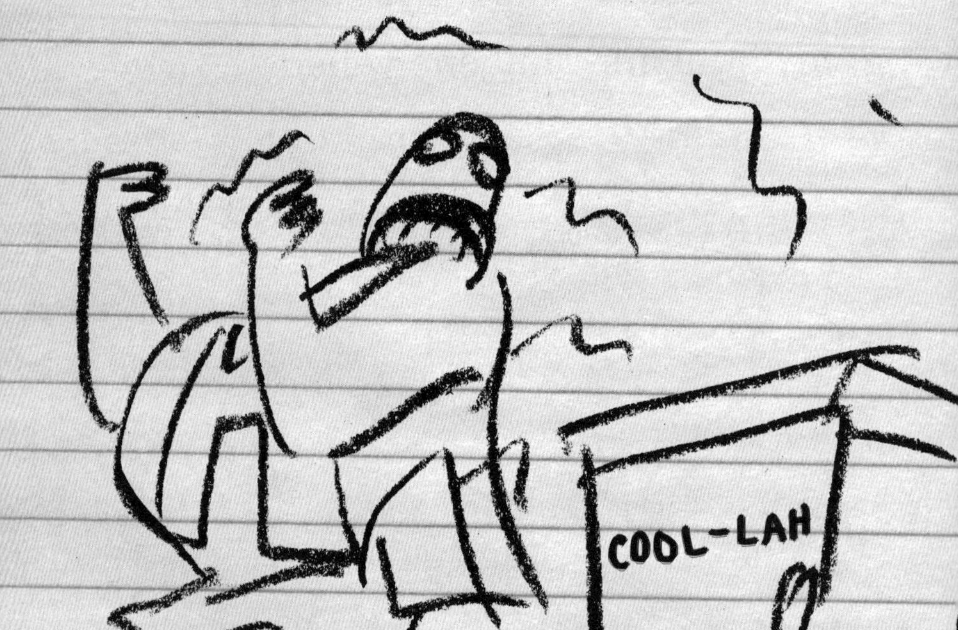


By Eugene

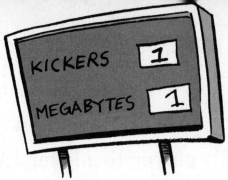

# The Westville Kickers: 1,

Sunnyview Megabytes: 1.

No matter what planet you were from or what language you spoke when you spoke of these things, there was no denying that the score was tied!

TIED!

And ties were really the only things that were made to be broken. Especially if Sunnyview was going to win its first game of the season.

The Kickers had the ball and brought it upfield, passing it from player to player like it was a hot potato traveling on a rocket.

George had recovered from his horrible "grass-facing" and he kicked the ball to his sister. Evan Mason raced between George and Lulu and tried to steal the ball. The ball hit his shin guards and knocked him over like a bowling pin.

**PLOP!**

Lulu ran in and dribbled the ball away. She bolted for the Sunnyview goal and passed the ball to Russell Tater. Sally Williams tried to block it.

She was fast. She was fearless. She missed the ball.

Russell passed it to George, and without slowing down, he smacked it with his right foot. It was over almost as soon as it began.

Goal.

SIGH.

Westville: 2, Sunnyview: 1. The tie score was history, thanks to the Morris twins, and Eugene felt a twisting knot in his stomach.

**BREET!**

And then the whistle blew.

HALFTIME.

The Megabytes headed to the bench, which Eugene and Bernie had been keeping warm for them. Eugene pulled Charlie from the

huddle. "Listen," he whispered to his best friend. "I've had a lot of time to . . . watch . . . the game and I discovered something pretty amazing."

"The soccer ball is a robot that's mind-controlled by the double-brain powers of the Morris twins?!" Charlie asked.

"Yes!" Eugene replied. "I mean, no. I mean, that's what I thought at first too, but then I noticed an ice cooler near their bench—"

Charlie turned to look.

"Don't look!" Eugene snapped. "They'll know we're on to them. I saw something like this before in Super Dude No. 26. Super Dude's powers were slowly being sucked away by El-Sucko!, who used a powerful sucking ray hidden in a wedge of stinky blue cheese to rob Super Dude of his powers.

"Baron and Baroness Von

Booger must be using an evil sucking thingie to zap Captain Awesome's awesome powers and make me, I mean him, trip over soccer balls."

Charlie gasped. "That was my *second* guess."

"If Captain Awesome is going to get back into the game and win it, I've gotta destroy whatever evil-sucking machine is in that cooler. It's stealing my powers!"

COOL-LAN

"What can I do?" Charlie asked.

"I need a distraction."

Before Eugene could say another word, both boys yelled, "Super Sonic Scream!"

"Good luck," Eugene said.

"Same to you," Charlie replied, and took a deep breath. "AAAA AAAAAAAAAAAAAAAAAAA AAAAAAAAAH!" the boy screamed and raced onto the soccer field waving his arms like a crazy duck who'd forgotten how to fly.

But the diversion was perfect! No one saw Captain Awesome superjump across the field and land atop the Westville Kickers' mysterious cooler of icy cold refreshments. . . .

COOL-LAH

# CHAPTER 8

## Showdown

By Eugene

KICKERS 2

MEGABYTES 1

"**I** know we're down two to one," Coach McGillicudy said at halftime. "But I'm really proud of the way you're all playing . . . and . . . um . . . sonic screaming."

That was just one of the many reasons Eugene loved his dad: no matter how busy he might be doing other things, he always made time to give a little look of thanks to his son's efforts to crush evil.

"The Westville Kickers may be

winning, but remember, the game isn't over until the final whistle," Coach McGillicudy continued. "And nobody unplugs the Megabytes!"

"*YEAH!*" Coach McGillicudy led the team in the team cheer that he'd written.

"Megabytes rah!
Megabytes yo!

Megabytes, Megabytes
Yo-ho-ho! High-five!"

The team high-fived.

*Thank goodness it wasn't Dinosaur Delmer singing "Monday,"* Eugene thought.

### BREET-TWEET-TWEET!

Halftime was over. Eugene headed back to the bench, but his dad tapped his shoulder.

"You're going the wrong way, Eugene."

"But the bench is that way," Eugene explained.

"I know, but the soccer field is *that* way. You do want to play, don't you?"

Eugene looked into his dad's eyes and his spirit soared! He gave his dad a quick hug, then raced onto the field, joining Charlie at midfield.

"I really wish I had my cape right now," Eugene whispered.

"I've been thinking about that," Charlie whispered back. "And you know what? That cape isn't Captain Awesome, *you* are. I mean, even without my Nacho Cheese Man outfit, *I* am *still* Nacho Cheese Man. I have all the powers of cheese in a can, not my superhero outfit."

As Eugene watched, Charlie scooted across the field and took control of the ball. "Cheesy-yo!" he yelled.

Nacho Cheese Man's classic battle cry startled the Morris twins, allowing Charlie to break past them and head for the Westville goal.

"Go, Nacho, go!" Eugene yelled and followed after him just in case someone accidentally passed him the ball now that he was no longer invisible.

Charlie slid his foot under the ball and blasted it into the air. The ball curved! It arced around goalie Bingo Swanson, and bounced into the goal.

*YEAH!*

Westville: 2, Sunnyview: 2.

*TIED!*

*AGAIN!*

But time was running out.

Then a thought shot into Eugene's mind: *Charlie's right! We're not superheroes because we wear superhero outfits! We wear superhero outfits because we're superheroes! I'm Captain Awesome with or without my cape, and I bet if I jumped as high as I can, I'd be able to leap over Baron and Baroness Von Booger and land in front of their goal! Then if anybody would just pass me the ball, it'd be an easy goal!*

Eugene crouched low and jumped as high as he could.

"MI-TEE!" he yelled as his feet left the ground.

WHAAAM!

The soccer ball smacked Eugene in the head.

**OUCH!**

As Eugene fell to the ground, it was as if the world started to move in s-l-o-w motion. The Megabytes and the Kickers watched as the soccer ball arced over the Von Booger twins' evil heads. They tried to block it, but really, who could ever jump as high as Captain Awesome?

The ball hit the ground, bounced once, sailed over Bingo's head and hit the back of the net.

*GOOOOOOOAAAAAL!*

**BREET-TWEET-TWEET!**

The clock ran out! The referee blew his whistle! The soccer game was over, and the Megabytes had won, 3–2!

"You did it, Eugene," Coach McGillicudy said, as he ran onto the field. "You scored the winning goal!"

"MI-TEE!" Charlie said, which made Eugene's smile even bigger.

"Nice going, Eugene!"

*Did Meredith really say something nice to me?! Wow. She even used my real name? That ball must've hit me so hard I'm hearing*

*things!* Eugene thought and rubbed his head.

The Megabytes raised Eugene on their shoulders and carried him off the field. The Morris twins stood in front of their goal, arms folded.

They were too stunned to move, or maybe they were waiting for their laser eyes to recharge.

It really didn't matter to Eugene either way. He was filled with a joy and happiness that couldn't be melted, even by the most zaptastic of lasers.

But there was still one more thing for Eugene to do. He had to keep the game ball out of the hands of the Von Boogers. That prize now belonged to Captain Awesome and his Megabytes, and he wasn't going to let anyone steal it from them.

"Come on, Nacho Cheese Man!" Captain Awesome yelled. "We've got one more goal to tend!" Captain

Awesome and Nacho Cheese Man ran toward the goal where the Von Boogers and the game ball waited. . . .

**YUM!**

The best thing about soccer, though, isn't the winning. It's going out for pizza after a game. Coach McGillicudy treated all the Megabytes to Jumbo Everything Pizzas from Jumbo's Pizza Palace.

Evan, Sally, Bernie, Meredith,

Mike, Marlo, and Charlie all agreed that Eugene would get the slice that had the most pepperoni.

And not only that, but Eugene managed to avoid the salad bar and not eat any of the green stuff.

*Does life get any better?*

Yes, it does.

Because on the drive home, Eugene's dad forgot to play any Dinosaur Delmer songs.

Both boys were eager to return to their neighborhood. They'd been gone for nearly two hours. Who knew how much eviling evil had been doing in their absence? Perhaps some horrible mutant monster from the sewer had gotten loose and started knocking over mailboxes or digging holes in people's yards.

"BUT"—Eugene began—"if there is no evil to be found . . . I mean, if EVERYTHING is absolutely, totally, completely normal, let's squeeze in a little soccer practice before our next Sunnyview Superhero Squad meeting."

"You took the cheese right out of my can!" Charlie replied.

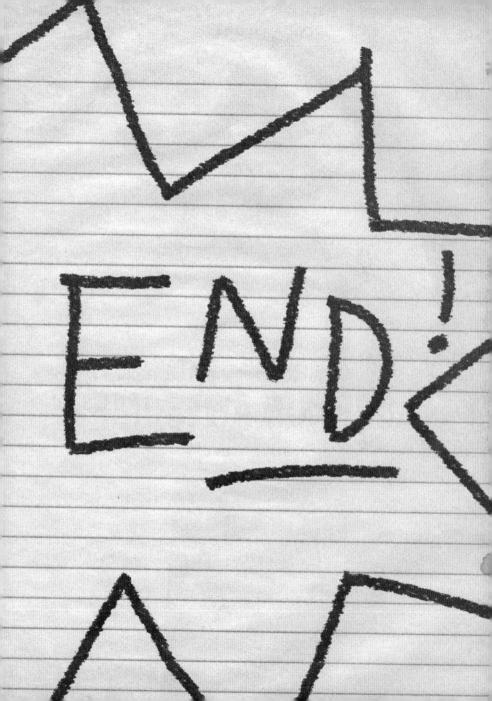

# CAPTAIN AWESOME SAVES THE WINTER WONDERLAND

*TING! TINGGG! TINGGGGG!*

"I love to play the triangle!" Eugene McGillicudy yelled out in a very heroic voice. In Mrs. Randle's music class, Eugene always went for the triangle. "I like any musical instrument that's shaped like pizza!"

*SHAKE! SHAKE-SHAKE!*

"Keep your triangle," Eugene's best friend, Charlie Thomas Jones, said. "I like the maracas. I don't know what's inside, but I hope it's dried bugs."

*SHAKE!*

Every Thursday morning,

Sunnyview Elementary School's music teacher, Mrs. Randle, passed out an assortment of xylophones, tambourines, recorders, cowbells, bongo drums, and more to all the second graders in her music room.

Eager students from different classes grabbed them like free chocolate, and sang and played under Mrs. Randle's waving baton.

"Cowbell!" cried Evan Mason as he grabbed one from the stack.

"The tambourine is MINE!" yelled Meredith Mooney, dressed in pink, from the ribbons in her hair to the shoelaces in her pink shoes. She had secretly stuck pink tape on the tambourine to mark it as her own.

Colin Boyle from Mrs. Duncan's second-grade class grabbed a set of bongo drums.

*BAMMITY-BAM! BAM!*

He bammed them with the palms of his hands. "Nice," he said.

"Okay, class," Mrs. Randle said. "Let's get started."

"And a one, and a two, and a one, two, three, four," she called out and swung her baton like she was swatting at a lazy fly.

*TING!*

*SHAKE!*

*TINGGG!*

*SHAKE-SHAKE!*

Eugene tinged and Charlie shook because superheroes step in front of danger and aren't afraid to make as much crazy loud music as possible. Just like that time Super Dude fought his musical enemy, Trouble Clef, and knocked the musical scales right off his slide trombone.

*KA-PUNCH!*